# storytime collection
# I Like to Read

# CONTENTS

# Let's Read

# At the Supermarket

Anna and Danny were going to the supermarket with their mother. They had invited their friend Dave to lunch. So they had to buy some things at the supermarket.

There were many people at the supermarket. Some people were buying fruits and vegetables, some were buying fish and meat, and others were buying bread, cakes and biscuits.

"Let's buy some fruits first," said Mother.

"Here are some apples, Mother," Anna said.

"And here are some lovely grapes," said Danny.

"Yes, children, let's buy some apples and grapes," Mother said. "Here are some bags for you. You may put the fruits in them. Anna, please go and get a trolley."

Danny put the grapes in his bag. Anna picked up some apples and put them in her bag.

Mother picked some juicy oranges and a pineapple and put them in the trolley.

"Children, put your bags in the trolley," said Mother. "Now, let's see. What else do I need? Oh yes, I need some bread."

They went to the counter that sold bread and cakes. Danny wanted to buy some cake and have it at once.

"No, Danny, you can't eat here," said Mother.

"But I'm hungry. I want to have some cake now," cried Danny.

"You're always feeling hungry," said Anna. "Didn't you have breakfast just now?"

"Stop that, children," Mother said. "Danny, you may have the cake after we go home. Come, let's choose some cake for you."

"I like strawberry cake, Mother," said Danny. "Please buy some strawberry cake for me."

Mother bought some bread, strawberry cake and biscuits and put them in the trolley.

"Mother, do you need vegetables?" asked Anna.

"Yes, Anna, I need some onions, potatoes, tomatoes and peas," Mother said. "Ah, here's a nice big cauliflower."

She picked up the cauliflower and put it in the trolley.

"Please buy some carrots, too," said Danny. "I love carrots."

Anna picked out the onions, potatoes and peas. Danny picked out some juicy tomatoes and carrots. The children put the vegetables into bags and put the bags in the trolley.

Then Mother picked up some chocolates and two cartons of pineapple juice.

"Come and choose some chips, children," she said. "Dave loves chips."

"Yippee!" said Danny. "Let's buy the cream and onion flavour."

"No, I think Dave likes the tomato flavour," said Anna.

"Take both the flavours," said Mother.

The children took the packets of chips and put them in the trolley.

At the next counter, people were buying ice cream.

"Dave loves ice cream, too, Mother," said Danny. "Let's buy some ice cream for him."

"Which flavour does he like?" Mother asked.

"Let's buy chocolate ice cream," said Anna.

"No, Dave likes strawberry ice cream," Danny said.

So Mother picked up some strawberry ice cream and put it in the trolley.

At the next counter, Mother picked up a tin of cheese.

"Shall we make pizza for Dave, children?" she asked.

"Oh yes, Dave loves pizza with lots of cheese," Anna said.

"We will help you make pizza, Mother," Danny said.

"And I shall bake a cake for Dave with Mother's help," said Anna.

"Let's see now, I need some tomato sauce and jam," said Mother.

She picked up a bottle of tomato sauce and a jar of jam and put them in the trolley.

Then she went to the next row and picked up three cakes of soap, some toothpaste and a bottle of shampoo.

"I need some milk and eggs, too," she said.

"I'll get them at once, Mother," Danny said. "I know where they are."

He ran to the next row and picked up two cartons of milk. He picked up a tray of eggs too.

"Look out, Danny, the eggs are going to fall!" Anna said, as she ran to help him.

"Thank you, Anna," said Danny.

"You must be more careful, Danny," she said.

"I know. I'm sorry," said Danny.

They went back with the milk and eggs to Mother.

"Now I need some medicines," said Mother. She went to the medicine counter.

Just then, Anna and Danny saw their friend Stella at the toy counter.

"Mother, there's Stella," said Anna. "May we go and talk to her?"

"Yes, dear," said Mother. "Come back here after meeting Stella."

"Hello, Stella," said Danny. "Are you buying any toys?"

"Yes, I'm looking for a nice toy for my sister," said Stella. "It's her birthday tomorrow. Can you help me choose a gift for her?"

"You can give her this train," said Danny.

"What about this doll? It is nice, too," said Anna.

"I know, Anna, but I gave her a doll on her last birthday. And she has a new train set. I like this car. I shall give her this car," said Stella.

The lady at the counter packed the toy. Stella thanked her and said goodbye to her friends.

Danny and Anna looked at the toys. There were some cars, a lovely teddy bear, a trumpet, a camera and many other toys.

Danny saw a drum set and tried to pull it out.

"Look out, Danny! The toys are going to fall!" said Anna.

Crash! The toys fell down.

"I'm so sorry," said Danny.

"Never mind," said the lady at the counter. "I hope you're not hurt. Do be more careful. You can help me pick up the toys."

Danny and Anna helped the lady pick up the toys and put them back.

Then the children went to look for their mother. They saw a little boy in the next row, sobbing loudly.

"What's the matter?" asked Anna.

"I'm I-I-lost. I can't f-f-find my mother," sobbed the little boy.

Anna told Danny to wait for her. She took the boy to the man at the ice-cream counter.

"This boy is lost," she said.

The man asked the boy his name. Then he and Anna took him down one row after another, looking for his mother.

Just then, a lady ran up to them and picked up the little boy.

"Where were you, son?" she said. "I've been looking everywhere for you. Now don't cry any more."

The little boy stopped crying and hugged his mother.

The lady thanked Anna and the man and bought her son an ice cream.

"Let me buy you an ice cream too, dear," she said to Anna.

"No, thank you. Mother has already bought ice cream. I must go back to my brother now," Anna said.

She went back to look for Danny.

Danny was standing near the side door of the supermarket. He was looking at a van parked there. The van was full of boxes.

Some men came with trolleys and put the boxes on them. Then they took the trolleys into the supermarket.

"Danny, what are you doing here?" asked Anna.

"Look, Anna, this is how all the things we buy come to the supermarket. The van brings them in these boxes," Danny said.

"Yes, Danny, I know," said Anna. "Now come along, Mother must be looking for us."

"There you are," said Mother. "I've got all the things I need. Now let's pay the bill and go home."

They went to the cash counter. There was a long line of people at the cash counter. Mother, Danny and Anna stood in line with the trolley. They were waiting for their turn to pay the bill.

Danny saw a magazine rack near the cash counter. He went to look at the magazines on it. He took out a comic and began to read it.

After reading the comic, he put it back on the rack. He picked up another book. As he turned to go and show it to his mother, he tripped and fell.

Crash! Some of the magazines fell from the rack.

"Are you hurt?" asked a man standing nearby.

"No, I'm all right," said Danny. "I must be more careful."

Mother rushed to Danny and helped him get up. They put back the magazines on the rack.

Then they went back to Anna, who was waiting with the trolley. Soon it was their turn to pay the bill.

"Now, children, help me take out all the things," said Mother.

Anna took out the medicines first.

"Here are the cartons of milk," Danny said, taking them out next.

Mother picked up the bread and the tray of eggs and put them on the counter. The man at the counter began making a bill for all the things.

"Now where are the cakes of soap and the shampoo?" asked Mother, looking in the trolley.

Danny looked carefully in the trolley and picked out the shampoo and cakes of soap.

"Here they are, Mother," he said. "And here's the toothpaste, too."

"Thank you, Danny," Mother said. "Now, let's see, here's the jam. And here's the ice cream and the cheese."

Anna took out the bottle of tomato sauce. Danny picked up the bag of carrots.

"Now let's take out the other vegetables," said Mother.

So Anna took out the peas, onions and tomatoes. Danny took out the cauliflower and potatoes and put them on the counter.

"Here's your cake, Danny," said Mother. "Once we reach home, you may eat it."

Anna took out the biscuits. Mother took out the chips, chocolates and juice. Then Danny took out the apples, oranges, pineapple and grapes.

"There, that's all," he said.

Mother paid the bill at the cash counter. The children helped her put all the things into some shopping bags.

Then they went out and put the bags into the car.

"That was fun!" said Anna.

"Yes," said Danny. "I do love going to the supermarket."

"Now let's go home and make lunch for Dave," said Mother.

Dave likes _strawberry_
ice cream.

(chocolate, vanilla,
strawberry)

Stella bought a _car_
for her sister.

(train, car, doll)

Danny loves _carrots_.

(carrots, potatoes,
peas)

# Let's Read

# Let's Have Lunch

"Mother, I'm off to Danny's house," called Dave. "Anna and Danny have invited me for lunch."

"Have a nice time, dear," his mother said. "When will you be back?"

"I'll be home by six o'clock," said Dave.

He walked to Danny's house and rang the bell. Danny's mother opened the door.

"Hello, Dave," she said. "How nice to see you! Please come in."

"Good morning, Mrs John," Dave said. "Mother said to say hello."

"We just got back from the supermarket," said Mrs John. "Danny and Anna have been helping me make pizzas and burgers for lunch."

As they walked into the hall, Anna came out of the kitchen. She was carrying a tray with a cake on it.

"Hello, Anna, have you been cooking?" asked Dave.

"Hello, Dave," said Anna. "Yes, Mother helped me to bake a cake."

"Mmm, it smells wonderful," said Dave.

Anna put the cake on the table.

"Where's Danny?" asked Dave.

"He must be in our room," said Anna. "But first come and see our new pet. It's a rabbit."

Anna took Dave to the back garden and showed him the rabbit.

"It's so sweet," said Dave.

"Father's friend Mr Ray gave it to us," said Anna.

Anna fed the rabbit some carrots and said, "Now let's go and find Danny."

Dave and Anna walked into the room, but they could not find Danny.

"Danny, where are you?" called Anna.

There was a small tent in the room.

"Maybe he's hiding in the tent," said Dave.

Just then Danny popped out of the tent with a toy pistol in his hand.

"Hands up!" he said to Dave.

Dave laughed and put his hands up.

"Isn't this tent lovely?" said Danny. "Uncle Toby got it for me as a birthday gift."

"Yes, it's very nice," said Dave.

"Let's play policeman and robbers," said Danny. "You have to steal this jewel box and hide it. Then you must hide, too. If I find you and the jewel box, then I win."

Danny went out of the room. Anna and Dave looked for a hiding place for the jewel box.

"We can hide the jewel box in the cupboard," said Anna. "No, wait a minute, he'll find it at once."

"Shall we hide it under the bed?" asked Dave.

"No, let's hide it behind these books," said Anna. "Hurry up, we have to hide, too."

They hid the jewel box behind some books. Then Anna hid behind the curtain on the window-sill. Dave hid inside the tent.

"We're ready, Danny," Anna said.

Danny came in. He saw the curtain on the window-sill move. He put up his toy pistol and said, "Hands up, Anna! Come out from behind the curtain."

Then Danny looked for Dave. He saw the tent move.

"Come out of the tent, Dave!" he said. "I know you're in there."

"So I've won the game," Danny said.

"No, you have to find the jewel box first," said Anna.

Danny looked under the bed and in the cupboard. Then he went over to Dave and began tickling him.

"Tell me where the jewel box is," he said, laughing.

Dave was very ticklish. He began laughing at once.

"Stop! Please stop!" he said. "I'll tell you. It's behind the books."

Danny took out the jewel box and said, "Now I've won the game."

"That's not fair," said Anna. "You made Dave tell you."

"Never mind, Anna," said Dave. "It was just a game. Now let's play basketball in the garden."

The children went into the garden to play basketball.

Dave dribbled the ball as he ran towards the basket. He threw the ball up and scored a basket.

"That was great!" said Anna. "You do play well, Dave."

Danny began dribbling the ball next, but Anna took it away from him and scored a basket.

"Yippee!" shouted Anna, and turned around. She bumped into Danny, who fell down.

"I'm sorry, Danny. Are you hurt?" said Anna.

"No, I'm fine," said Danny.

They played for some more time. Anna scored the most baskets. She enjoyed playing basketball.

"I'm tired," said Danny. "I can't play any more."

"Yes, let's rest now," Dave said.

"It will be cool under that tree," said Anna. "I'll get a sheet from the house to sit on."

Danny and Dave helped Anna spread the sheet.

They sat on the sheet under the tree. Mrs John brought them some sandwiches, biscuits and juice.

"Thank you, Mother," said Danny. "We are all so thirsty."

The children drank plenty of juice and munched on the biscuits.

"Mmm, that was wonderful!" said Dave. "I was so thirsty."

"Yes, I was thirsty, too," said Danny. "It's so hot outside."

"Let's go and play inside now," said Anna. "It will be cooler."

"What shall we play?" asked Dave.

"Let's have a car race with our toy cars," said Danny.

They went to the children's room and set up a racing track with sheets of cardboard.

"Are you ready to race?" asked Anna.

"Yes, let's go," said Dave and Danny.

Vroom! Vroom! The children raced their cars along the racing track.

"Yippee! I've won the race," said Dave.

Then they played snakes and ladders. Danny was lucky with the dice and soon he won the game.

"Children, it's time for lunch now," called Mrs John.

"Yippee! I'm hungry," Danny shouted, and raced to the table.

"You're always feeling hungry," said Anna.

"Wow! Pizzas and burgers and chips!" said Dave. "All my favourite food."

"I helped Mother make the pizzas," said Danny. "I put lots of cheese. You like cheese, don't you, Dave?"

"Oh yes, I love cheese," said Dave.

"And I helped Mother make the burgers," said Anna.

"The pizza is very tasty," said Dave. "And this burger is lovely too."

The children talked about their friends in school as they had lunch.

After lunch, the children watched television. Mrs John brought them some strawberry ice cream.

"Mmm! Strawberry ice cream!" said Dave. "Thank you, Mrs John. Strawberry is my favourite flavour."

"I know," said Danny. "I told Mother at the supermarket, didn't I?"

"Yes, dear, you did," laughed Mother.

It was time for cartoon shows on television. Danny wanted to see *Tom and Jerry,* his favourite cartoon show.

"You see that every day," said Anna. "Dave, what would you like to watch?"

Dave said that he loved to watch *Superman.* So they all watched the *Superman* show.

When the show was over, the children began reading books. All of them enjoyed reading.

Dave found a comic book that he liked. Danny took out his favourite book on aeroplanes.

Anna's friend Clare had given her a new book to read. She took it out and began to read it.

"Anna, did you feed the rabbit?" Mother asked.

"Yes, Mother, I fed the rabbit some carrots when I took Dave to see it," said Anna.

Just then, the bell rang. The children raced to the door to see who had come. It was Clare.

"Hello, Clare," said Anna. "I was just reading the book you gave me."

"Hello, Anna," said Clare. "I've come to give you your bag. You left it behind at my house."

"Thank you, Clare," said Anna.

"I'm so glad you've come, Clare," said Danny. "Let's go and play in the park now."

"Yes, we can play football with our other friends," said Anna.

The children ran about the park, passing the ball to each other and trying to score goals.

Danny got the ball and passed it to Clare. She kicked the ball high and scored a goal. Then Dave got the ball. He passed it to Anna. As she tried to kick it, she bumped into Clare, who fell down.

"Clare, are you hurt?" asked Dave.

"No, I'm fine. My leg just hurts a bit," said Clare.

"I'm so sorry, Clare," said Anna.

"Never mind. I'm fine now," Clare said. "Let's play."

The children played for some time. Soon they were tired and thirsty.

"Let's go home now," said Danny.

Mrs John gave the children cake, biscuits and sandwiches for tea.

"Clare, do you know, Anna baked this cake," said Dave.

"It's very nice," said Clare.

After tea, Dave and Clare thanked Anna, Danny and Mrs John and went home.

"Thank you, Mother," said Anna and Danny. "We had a lovely time today."

Danny popped _out_ (in, out) of the tent with a toy pistol _in_ (in, under) his hand.

The children had _pizzas_ for lunch. (pizzas, rice, chow mein)

They played _basketball_ in the garden. (football, basketball, tennis)

# Let's Read

# A Shopping Trip

As soon as lunch was over, Mother asked Neil and Nora to get ready.

"Where are we going, Mother?" asked Neil.

"Don't you remember? We are going shopping for our trip to the mountains," said Nora.

"Oh yes! Now I remember," said Neil. "Grandpa and Grandma will be coming along too. What fun we shall have! But why are we going shopping so soon? The holidays are still a few days away."

"I know, Neil, but we can't do all our shopping in one day. So we'll buy some of the things on our lists today," said Mother.

They got ready quickly and went to the car.

"Have you got your shopping lists, children?" asked Mother.

"Yes, Mother," said Neil.

"Then read out your lists, so that I know which shops to go to," said Mother.

"Oh, Neil, do let me read out my list first," said Nora.

"All right," said Neil.

"This is what I have on my list, Mother," said Nora.

She began reading out from her list. "Chocolates, chips, candy, books, shoes, woollen socks, wool and knitting needles . . ."

She stopped as Neil began giggling.

"Why are you giggling, Neil?" she asked.

"Wool and knitting needles!" said Neil. "Why do you need those? Are you going to sit and knit like Grandma? How silly!"

"You are the one who is being silly, Neil," said his mother. "Nora is buying the wool and knitting needles for Grandma. I think it's very nice of her to remember to buy things for Grandma."

Soon they were at the market.

"I've remembered to make a note in my list to buy magazines for you and laces for Father's shoes," said Neil.

"That's nice of you, dear," said his mother with a smile. "Now read out your list."

"Cake, juice, magazines, shoelaces, biscuits, fruit, football and a pack of playing cards," said Neil, reading out from his list.

"All right, let's go to the bookstall first. It's right here," said Mother.

They bought some magazines and books at the bookstall.

"Shall we buy a sports magazine for Grandpa?" asked Neil.

"Yes, Neil, that would be nice," said his mother.

They went to the shoe shop next.

"What kind of shoes would you like to see?" asked the man in the shop.

"Please show us some sports shoes," said Mother.

Neil chose a pair of black and white sports shoes. Nora walked around the shop, looking at all the shoes.

"I like these green shoes," said Nora.

"I'm sorry. We don't have those in your size," said the man.

"Never mind, dear," said her mother. "These red and blue ones look nice, too."

"Mother, we have to buy shoelaces for Father and woollen socks for all of us," said Neil.

"Yes, thank you, dear," said his mother.

They put their shopping bags in the car and went to the store on the opposite side.

Mother took out her list and picked up some cakes of soap, toothpaste, a bottle of shampoo and tomato sauce. She remembered that there was no milk at home. She picked up some cartons of milk and a tray of eggs.

Neil and Nora were getting tired of waiting for their mother to pick up all the things on her list.

"I have an idea," said Nora.

"Mother, shall we choose our snacks while you pick up the things on your list?"

"Yes, that's a good idea," said Mother. "It will save some time."

The children chose some of their favourite chips, juices, chocolates, candy and cakes.

"What kind of biscuits do you want, Neil?" asked Nora.

"My favourite flavour is chocolate," said Neil. "Let's buy these chocolate biscuits."

They took the snacks to Mother. She paid for all the things and they took the bags to the car.

"I'm so excited," said Nora. "It's such fun shopping for our trip to the mountains."

After they had put away the bags, Nora remembered that she wanted to buy stamps at the post office.

"Mother, may we stop by at the post office? I'd like to buy some stamps and envelopes. I want to write to my friends and tell them all about our holiday," she said.

"Girls! All they want to do is read books and write letters," said Neil. "I've never seen such . . ."

"Stop that at once, Neil," said Mother. "Yes, Nora, we'll stop at the post office. You may pick up your stamps and envelopes there."

The children and their mother went to the post office.

Nora saw a long line of people waiting at the counter that sold stamps.

She told her mother, "This will take some time, Mother. There's such a long line. Shall we come back another day to pick up the stamps and envelopes?"

"Yes, let's do that," said Neil quickly.

"No, let's wait in line," said Mother.

"I'm sure it won't take long. Don't worry, Nora, there's plenty of time to do all our shopping."

They waited in line till it was their turn. Nora asked the man at the stamp counter for some stamps and envelopes.

The man smiled at her and said, "So many envelopes? How many letters are you going to write?"

"We shall be going on a trip to the mountains," said Nora. "I want to write to my friends and tell them all about our trip."

"A trip to the mountains!" said the man. "That's nice. I do wish I could go too."

Nora smiled and said, "When I get back, I'll tell you all about my trip."

Next they went to the wool shop. At the wool shop, Mother, Nora and Neil looked at all the balls of wool, trying to choose what colour of wool to buy.

"Nora, which colour will Grandma like?" asked Neil.

"I don't know, Neil. All these colours are so lovely. I wish we could buy them all," said Nora.

After looking at the coloured balls of wool for a long time, Nora shut her eyes and picked up a ball of wool. It was purple in colour.

"Mother, let's buy this," she said. "I'm sure Grandma will like it."

"Yes, that's a lovely colour," said Mother. She bought some purple wool and knitting needles for Grandma.

"Let's see now, what's left?" said Mother, looking at her list. "Oh, we have to buy a jacket for Father."

"Father wants a sports jacket with many pockets," said Neil.

"Mother, remember to buy a jacket with a zip. Father always loses the buttons of his jacket," said Nora.

"That's a good idea," said her mother with a smile.

The jacket shop was opposite the wool shop. They looked at the jackets hanging in the show window. Then they went into the shop and began looking at all the jackets.

"This jacket is nice, Mother," said Neil. "It has many pockets."

"Yes," said Nora. "It has a zip too. I like this jacket. Let's buy it."

Mother bought the jacket for Father.

By now Neil was tired. He was hungry too.

"Let's stop for some snacks and ice cream," said Mother.

"What a great idea!" said Neil and Nora at once.

They stopped at a coffee shop for some sandwiches and ice cream.

While they were having their ice cream, Neil saw a lady rushing past the window, waving her hands and shouting.

He ran out to see what was happening. He heard her shouting, "Stop! Thief! He has taken my bag!"

Mother and Nora ran out after Neil. They saw a man running away with a bag in his hand.

"Quick, Nora! Come with me," said Neil, as he raced the other way.

"Wait, children!" said Mother, as she ran after them.

"Why are we going this way?" asked Nora as they ran.

"The road takes a turn and comes back this way," said Neil. "We can try to stop the thief when he passes by here."

The children hid behind the door of a shop.

"Neil, when the thief passes by, throw the marbles that you have on the road," said Nora.

"Good idea!" said Neil. He took out some marbles from his pocket and threw them on the road. As the thief passed by, he slipped on the marbles and fell. The bag slipped out of his hand.

"Catch him! He's a thief!" shouted the children.

Some people passing by caught the thief. They picked up the bag and gave it back to the lady.

"Thank you," she said.

"You should thank these two children," said a man.

"How did you stop the thief from running away?" asked another man.

"My sister told me to throw some marbles in his way," said Neil. "When he was passing us, I threw the marbles and he slipped and fell."

"That was very clever and brave of you," said the lady. "Thank you, children. Come, let me buy you both an ice cream."

"But we just had an ice cream!" said the children.

"Never mind, I'm sure you would like another one," laughed the lady.

Just then, Mother ran up to them.

"Are you all right, children?" she asked.

"Oh yes, Mother. We helped to catch the thief," said Neil.

"Next time, don't just run away like that," she said. "You may get hurt."

"I'm sorry, Mother," said Neil, as he hugged her.

"I am sorry too," said Nora.

"Your children are very brave and clever," the lady said to Mother. "I'd like to buy them an ice cream to thank them for helping to catch the thief and getting my bag back."

Neil and Nora thanked the lady for the ice cream.

"Let's go back home now," said Mother. "We can do the rest of our shopping another day."

They got into the car and went home.

"We must tell Father all about our shopping trip," said Nora.

"And I shall tell him how we helped to catch a thief," said Neil.

Ans: The mother bought a purple wool for grandma.

## What did Mother buy for Grandma?

Ans: The children ate Ice-Cream at the coffee shop.

## What did the children eat at the coffee shop?

Ans: The children threw marbles when the theif was passing

## How did the children help to catch the thief?

throug them & the theif fell down.

# Let's Read

# A Visit to Grandma's

It was a bright, sunny day. Kim ran into the garden and called out to her mother, "I'm ready, Mother! Let's go. It's such a lovely sunny day."

Mother came to the doorway, carrying a basket.

"Take this out to the car, dear," she said. "I've packed some food for Grandma and Grandpa."

Kim took the basket from Mother.

"Mmm, something smells good!" said Paul, as he came down the stairs.

"I've baked a cake for Grandma and a pie for Grandpa," said Mother.

"What about us?" said Paul. "It's a long way to Grandpa's farm, and we'll be hungry after a while."

"There are snacks for you, too," laughed Mother.

Father was outside, putting their bags into the car. Kim gave him the basket and they all got in.

"Kim, did you remember to pack Grandma's wool and knitting needles?" asked Mother.

"Yes, Mother, they are in my bag," said Kim. "I shall tell Grandma to knit me a woollen scarf. Maybe it will be ready before our trip to the mountains."

Grandpa and Grandma lived on a farm far away from the city. They had a large house with two pet dogs called Bimbo and Sheba and a pet cat called Cleo. They had also got a pet tortoise a few days ago.

Kim and Paul loved to visit them and play with the pets. Grandpa also had four horses in his stables. Kim loved horses, and she went riding at the farm every day.

"I wonder how big Bimbo has grown," said Paul. "He was such a naughty little dog when we saw him on our last visit."

"But Sheba was a darling," said Kim. "Remember how she used to snuggle up in our blankets last winter?"

"Yes, and Grandma would come and scold us for letting her into our beds," laughed Paul.

"Children, this time you must help Grandma and Grandpa on the farm," said Father. "You are old enough now, and they need help on the farm."

"Oh yes, Father, don't worry," said Kim. "I shall help Grandma feed the hens and collect the eggs. I love playing with the sweet little chicks."

"And I shall help Grandpa feed the horses and clean the stables," said Paul.

"Are you going to learn how to ride a horse this time, Paul?" asked Kim with a naughty smile.

"Yes, I am," said Paul. "I shall tell Grandpa to teach me how to ride a horse."

On their visit to the farm some weeks ago, Paul had not gone near the stables at all. He was frightened of horses.

But his best friend Ray loved horses. Ray showed Paul how to feed the pony they had at school. Soon Paul learned to play with the pony and was not frightened any more.

"You can learn to ride on Robbie," said Nora. "He's so gentle."

By now they had left the city far behind. The cool breeze blowing through the window made Paul and Kim sleepy. After a while both of them fell asleep.

Suddenly, Paul woke up and said, "I'm hungry. Mother, where is the food you packed for us?"

They all stopped for a while and had some sandwiches and juice.

When they drove into the farm, they found Grandma waiting for them. Kim jumped out of the car and ran to greet her.

The two dogs, Bimbo and Sheba, ran around, barking happily. Paul got down and tried to pick up Bimbo. But he was too big now for Paul's little hands. Bimbo licked Paul's face and barked.

Grandpa came out to greet them.

"Hello, Paul, Kim, how big you've grown!" said Grandpa, as he hugged both of them.

"Hello, Grandpa. Let's go and look around the farm," said Paul.

"There will be time enough for that later," said Grandma. "Come in and rest for a while."

"Grandma, we've brought your knitting needles and wool," said Kim. "Will you knit a woollen scarf for me? I want to wear it when we go to the mountains."

"Yes, dear, I will. Now come and put your bags in your room," she said.

As they walked into the living room, Paul tripped over something on the floor and fell.

"Oh, I'm so sorry, Paul! Are you hurt?" said Grandpa, as he helped Paul to get up. "It's that silly Oliver. He's always in the way."

"Oliver? Who's that?" asked Kim at once.

"Oliver is a tortoise. He's our new pet. I told you

about him last week, didn't I?" said Grandpa. "Look, there he goes!"

The children turned around to see a tortoise slowly walking along the floor.

"Oh, he's so sweet," said Kim, as she bent down to look at him. "Grandpa, will he be frightened and run away if I touch him?"

"Tortoises can't run, silly! They only walk," said Paul.

"I know that," said Kim.

"When Oliver is frightened, he tucks his head into his shell," said Grandpa. "That's how I found him. He had fallen into a pit and could not get out. I thought he was a stone till I saw him move. He looked so lost and frightened that I brought him home."

Kim stroked Oliver's shell.

"He's so gentle," she said.

"Grandpa, where's Cleo? I can't see her anywhere," said Paul.

"She must be on her favourite tree," said Grandpa. "She has become fat and very lazy."

Paul went out to look for Cleo, the pet cat.

"Cleo, where are you? Miaow, miaow," he said, trying to mew like the cat.

He saw Cleo sitting on the branch of a tree.

"There you are!" said Paul. "Cleo, Grandpa was right. You have become fat and lazy."

The fat cat mewed softly and licked her lips.

"Lunch is ready, children," said Grandma. "Wash up and come to the table."

There were plenty of goodies for lunch. Father took a large helping of his favourite roast potatoes while Mother helped herself to some salad. There were pizzas for the children too.

"Mmm, thank you for baking my favourite pie," said Grandpa, as he helped himself to a large slice.

In the evening, the children went to the stables. Kim went for a ride on her favourite horse named Silver.

The next day, Paul ran to Grandpa to begin his riding lesson. At first he was a little frightened, but he soon began to enjoy himself. Grandpa showed him how to ride Robbie, the gentle pony.

Paul quickly learned how to ride and was soon riding all over the farm.

"This is fun, Grandpa!" he said. "When I go back to school, I shall show my friends that I can ride."

Kim went with Grandma to the pens. First she helped Grandma feed the hens. Then she carefully collected the eggs from each pen and put them in a large basket.

"Thank you, Kim," said Grandma. "You've been a great help."

"I enjoyed it, Grandma," said Kim. "I love to come here and play with the sweet little chicks. I shall come and help you every day."

That night, Grandpa and Father cooked dinner.

"Please pass me an egg," Father said to Grandpa as he stirred the stew.

"Here you are. Oops!" Grandpa dropped the egg.

Father laughed and said, "Never mind. We'll clean up later."

After Grandpa and Father had finished cooking, the children helped them clean up. Then they sat down to dinner.

Father and Grandpa had made baked vegetables and salad and stew.

"That was a good dinner," said Kim.

"Now let's have the cake Mother baked for Grandma," said Paul.

The next day, Paul ran off for his riding lesson with Grandpa. After the lesson, Grandpa taught Paul how to feed the horses and clean the stables.

"I wish Ray could see me now," Paul said to Grandpa. "I don't know why I was so frightened of horses. They are so gentle, and my pony Robbie is a darling."

Every morning, Kim helped Grandma feed the hens and collect the eggs. Paul helped Grandpa clean the stables and feed the horses. Then the children played ball with the dogs and went for long walks on the farm with their father and mother.

After lunch, everyone rested for a while. Then they played games or watched television together.

The children were enjoying their visit to Grandma's, but soon it was time to go back.

"We have been here for a week, but I feel like we came here just a day ago," said Paul, as he hugged Robbie for the last time.

"Yes, I know," said Kim, stroking Oliver's shell. "I wish we didn't have to go so soon."

"Never mind, children," said Grandpa. "We'll be seeing you again soon."

"Yes, all of us are going on a trip to the mountains, remember?" said Grandma.

"Oh yes!" said Paul, as he and Kim hugged Grandpa and Grandma. "Bye, we'll see you again soon."

Mother and Father also said goodbye to Grandma and Grandpa and they drove away.

"That was fun!" said Kim.

"Yes," said Paul. "I hope we can visit Grandma and Grandpa again soon."

Ans- Grandma scolded Kim and Paul because they let the pet dogs into their bed.

**Why did Grandma scold Kim and Paul?**

**How did Paul help Grandpa?**

(a) He washed the car.

(b) He fed the horses and cleaned the stables.

(c) He bathed the cat.

**How did Kim help Grandma?**

(a) She bathed the dogs.

(b) She cooked the food.

(c) She fed the hens and collected the eggs.

# Let's Read

# A Summer Holiday

Ruby and Ted's summer holiday had just begun. They were very excited as they were going to spend a few days at a hill station.

"Father, we're ready to go," shouted Ruby.

"Yes, our suitcase is packed and ready. What about yours?" said Ted.

"This suitcase just won't shut," panted Father. "Come and help me shut it, children."

The suitcase was packed with woollens. The children sat down on it and bounced up and down, laughing all the while, until Father was able to shut it.

"Whew! That was quite a job. Thank you, children," said Father.

Mother came in and said, "I'm ready now."

"Father, have you packed the camera?" asked Ruby.

"Yes, dear," said Father, as he took the suitcase out to the car.

"Mother, where are the snacks?" asked Ted.

"Jean is just packing them," said Mother. "Why don't you go to the kitchen and help her?"

Jean was their old housekeeper. Ted went into the kitchen and began helping her.

"Don't forget the chips and juice, Jean," said Ted.

"I've already packed them, dear," said Jean with a smile. "Will you miss me, Ted?"

"Oh yes, Jean, I'll miss you. But we'll be back soon," said Ted.

Father put the bags in the boot of the car and they all got in.

"Hooray! We're off at last," shouted Ted, jumping up and down in the back seat.

"How long will it take to reach, Mother?" asked Ruby.

"I'm not sure, but I think it will take about four hours to reach the hill station," said Mother.

They waved a cheerful goodbye to Jean.

"Goodbye, children," said Jean. "Take care and have a nice time."

"Goodbye, Jean, we'll miss you," said the children.

"I'll miss you, too," said Jean as she waved to them. "Make sure you take plenty of photographs of the hill station."

As they drove away, Ted saw his friend Benny on his bicycle.

"Goodbye, Benny, we're going on a summer holiday," he shouted.

"Goodbye, Ted, have a nice time," said Benny. "I shall be going on a holiday next week. I'll see you when you get back."

"Yes," said Ted. "We'll show you photographs of the hill station."

Soon they had left the town far behind. All around them there were fields of corn and wheat. The crops swayed in the breeze.

Ruby rolled down her window and listened to the wind rushing past.

After some time, the children began to feel hungry.

"May we stop for a while and have some snacks?" asked Ted. "I'm hungry."

"Yes. I'm hungry, too," said Ruby.

Father stopped the car near a grassy spot and they took out the snacks.

Jean had packed sandwiches, chips, cake and lemonade. As they ate, they looked around them. A farmer was driving a red tractor in a field nearby.

A bus full of schoolchildren went past them. The schoolchildren waved at Ted and Ruby, and they waved back.

"We're going on a summer holiday," shouted Ruby.

When they had finished eating, Father said, "Children, please help me clear up. Pick up the crumbs and bits of food lying around. We must not litter the place."

"Yes, Father," said the children.

Mother packed the leftover food. The children picked up the crumbs and bits of food. A little bird was hopping around nearby.

"Let's give these crumbs to that little bird," said Ruby. "It must be hungry."

They put the crumbs and bits of food below a tree. The bird flew to it at once and began pecking at the crumbs.

"Isn't it sweet?" said Ruby.

A crow was sitting on that tree. It saw the bird pecking at the crumbs. It flew down and began cawing loudly. The little bird was frightened and flew away.

"Shoo," said Ted, trying to frighten the crow. "Don't take the little bird's food, you greedy crow."

The crow cawed loudly again, flapped its wings and flew straight at Ted.

He got frightened and cried out, "Mother!"

Mother shooed away the crow. Ted covered his face and began to cry.

"Don't cry, Ted. The crow has gone," said Ruby. "Mother has shooed it away."

Mother hugged Ted and took him back to the car.

As they were getting into the car, Mother said to Father, "Let me drive for a while now. Then you can get some rest."

So Father leaned back in his seat, switched on the car radio and shut his eyes.

After a while Ruby said, "Look over there, I can see the mountains!"

"Where?" asked Ted excitedly.

"There," she said, pointing out of the window.

"I want to take some photographs of the mountains," said Father. "Let's stop here for a while."

Mother parked the car on the side of the road. Father got out with the camera and took some photographs. Then they got back into the car.

Soon they had begun climbing the mountain. The road was narrow and winding and the car turned this way and that around the sharp curves. Ruby began to feel sick. There was a funny feeling in her stomach and she had a headache.

"Mother, please stop," she said.

"What is it, dear?" asked Mother, as she stopped the car on the side of the road.

"I feel sick," said Ruby, getting out of the car.

"Walk around for a while. You'll feel better," said Father.

Mother gave her a tablet.

"Here, take this tablet, dear. It's for mountain sickness," she said.

Ruby took the tablet and then splashed some cold water on her face and neck.

"I feel better now," she said.

They got back into the car and Mother took care to drive slowly.

They passed a school. Little children in colourful clothes were playing in the playground. Mother stopped the car near the school. Ruby got down with the camera and took some photographs.

They reached the hill station around noon. Their hotel faced the valley.

The children got out and looked around them.

"It's so beautiful," said Ruby.

"And so quiet. You can even hear the wind in the trees," said Mother, as she got out.

"I am hungry again," said Ted.

"But you just ate some time ago," said Ruby.

"Mountain air makes us hungry more often," said Mother with a smile. "Now help us take the bags to the rooms."

As soon as they had put away their bags in their rooms, Ted ran out to the playground.

"Ted, I thought you were hungry," said Mother.

"I'll play for some time and then eat," he called out. "Coming, Ruby?"

"I'll just have a wash and come," said Ruby.

She washed her face and hands. Then she ran out to the playground.

"What shall we play?" asked Ruby.

"Look, here's a swing!" said Ted.

Ted and Ruby played on the swing for a while. Then they found a rubber ball and began playing with it.

"Here, Ted, catch," said Ruby, as she threw the ball.

But Ted could not catch the ball. It bounced down the side of the mountain.

"There, now it's lost," said Ruby.

They went to the edge of the mountain and looked down.

"Look! There's the ball. It's bouncing past those bushes," said Ted.

A village boy had been watching them play. He saw the ball bouncing down. He ran down the side of the mountain, searched among the bushes and got the ball out.

"Thank you," said Ruby and Ted, as he handed them the ball.

"What's your name?" asked Ted.

"Joe," said the boy shyly.

"Please come and play with us tomorrow," said Ruby. "We will be staying here for a few days. It will be nice to have someone to play with."

The boy nodded his head, smiled shyly and ran away.

Every morning Ted and Ruby played in the playground till their mother and father got ready. After that, all of them went for long walks along the narrow mountain roads.

Ruby loved the wild flowers growing on the side of the mountain. Every day, she picked a bunch of them and put them in a vase in her room.

One day, when Ruby was plucking some wild flowers, she touched a leaf and her hands began to itch.

"Oh Mother," she cried. "My hands are itching and hurting."

A villager was passing by. He quickly plucked a leaf from a nearby tree.

"Here, rub this leaf on your hands. They will stop itching," he said.

Ruby rubbed the leaf and felt better at once.

"Thank you," she said.

Mother and Father thanked the villager too.

"You must be careful while plucking wild flowers," said the villager, and went away.

Sometimes, they walked to the village. There they watched the villagers doing their daily work.

The village boy soon became good friends with Ruby and Ted. Every day, he brought along a few of his friends and all the children played together.

The village children showed Ruby and Ted how to climb trees and pluck juicy fruit.

"This is fun," Ruby said. "We must show our friends back home how to climb trees."

One day, Mother and Father took Ruby and Ted to the village handicraft shop where they bought gifts for their grandparents, for Jean and their friends.

"Let's buy these caps for Benny and Susie," said Ted.

"Yes, they are nice," Ruby said. Father bought a belt for Grandpa. Mother bought a blouse for Grandma and a scarf for Jean.

They also took some photographs of the village and the friends they had made there.

The days flew past. Soon it was time to go back home.

On the drive back home, everyone was very quiet. They were sad that their holiday had come to an end.

But when they reached home, the children rushed to Jean and began to tell her all about their holiday.

"Look, Jean, here's the scarf Mother bought for you," said Ruby. "Isn't it pretty?"

"Yes, it is. Thank you so much," said Jean.

The children spent the rest of their holidays telling their friends about the wonderful time they had at the hill station.

They showed them the photographs and told them about the friends they had made in the village.

"I shall never forget this lovely holiday," said Ruby.

"Mother, can we go back there again next year?" said Ted.

"We'll see, dear," said Mother with a smile.

How did the children shut the suitcase?

Why was Ted frightened?

Who helped the children get their ball back?

# Let's Read

# At the Beach

Vicky and Dina were very excited. It was the first day of their holidays.

"Where do you want to go today, children?" asked Mother.

"To the beach," they shouted.

"All right, go and get your things," said Mother.

The children helped Mother pack the beach bag. They packed the beach towel, some napkins, a pail, a spade, a beach ball, some snacks and a rubber bone for Terry, their dog.

Terry saw his bone being packed and knew he was going too. He ran around them, wagging his tail and barking. He was very excited.

"Terry, stop running around. You're getting in the way," said Dina.

Soon they were at the beach.
They walked along the shore
slowly.

"Look at the sea! It's so blue!"
said Vicky.

"And look at these lovely
seashells," said Dina.

"Where shall we sit, children?"
asked Mother.

"Let's sit here. The sand is just
right for making sandcastles," said Vicky.

Vicky took out the towel and began to spread it on
the sand.

"No, Terry, don't pull the towel," said Dina.

But naughty Terry wagged his tail and ran away
with the towel in his
mouth.

Vicky ran after him,
shouting, "Come
back at once, you
naughty dog!"

Terry ran faster and
Vicky ran after him.

Suddenly, Terry turned around and ran back to Mother. He dropped the towel at her feet.

"That was naughty of you, Terry," said Mother.

Terry hung his head.

Woof! Woof! he barked softly.

Vicky came back, panting.

"Silly dog," he said. "You made me run for nothing."

"He thought it was a game," said Mother, smiling as she put the towel away.

"Here's a nice game for you," said Vicky. He took Terry's rubber bone out of the beach bag and threw it as far as he could. At once, Terry wagged his tail and ran after it, barking and panting.

Mother found a deck chair and sat down on it.

"I shall sit here in the sun and read," she said, putting on her hat and sunglasses.

"Shall we build a sandcastle first?" asked Vicky.

"Yes," said Dina. "You take the spade and dig up the sand. I'll get some water from the sea."

Vicky and Dina took out their things from the bag. Dina washed the pail in the sea water.

"Be careful, Dina," said Mother. "Don't go too far out into the sea."

"Yes, Mother, I'll be careful," said Dina.

She filled the pail with water and took it to Vicky.

"I've dug up a lot of sand. Let's build our sandcastle now," said Vicky.

The children mixed sand and water and began building the sandcastle. Soon it was ready.

"It looks good, doesn't it?" said Vicky proudly.

"Yes, but … I know! We must put some seashells on it," said Dina.

She placed some seashells on the sandcastle and put flags on top.

Terry saw Vicky digging up the sand. When the sandcastle was ready, he got his rubber bone and began digging around the sandcastle.

"Stop that at once, you naughty dog!" said Dina.

Terry stopped digging and hung his head, barking softly.

"He thinks it's a game," laughed Mother. "He wants to hide his bone in your sandcastle."

"Whew! I'm thirsty now," said Vicky.

"Come, let's have some juice," said Mother.

She spread out the towel under a beach umbrella and gave the children some juice.

Terry was very excited. Woof! Woof! he barked as he ran along the shore. Sometimes he chased the birds too.

"There are so many birds here, Mother," said Vicky.

"Yes, Vicky. The birds come here looking for food. Many people come to the beach, and they bring food with them. The birds fly around, looking for the food they leave behind," said Mother.

"Ah, food!" said Dina. "Let's have some food too."

"Here, children, have some chips. You must be hungry," said Mother.

The children munched on chips as they looked around them.

"Mother, look at that lighthouse," said Dina.

"What is a lighthouse?" asked Vicky.

"It is a tower with a strong light. It guides ships to the shore and warns them about any rocks in the sea," said Mother.

Suddenly Terry ran up and began pulling at the towel.

"Stop that at once, you naughty dog!" said Dina.

"No, Dina, Terry is a smart dog," said Mother. "Look, the sea water has wet our towel. Terry was trying to warn us."

"Smart Terry," said Vicky, as Terry wagged his tail proudly.

"Mother, come and play with us now," said Vicky.

He took the beach ball and threw it at Dina, saying, "Here, Dina, catch!"

Dina caught the ball and threw it at Mother.

"Oops! Missed it," said Mother.

The ball rolled away and Terry wagged his tail and ran after it, barking happily.

Every time he tried to catch the big ball with his paws, it rolled away.

"Silly dog," said Vicky, laughing. "Why don't you play with your rubber bone?"

He threw the rubber bone as far as he could. Terry ran after it at once.

The children played ball with their mother for a while.

"Oh, look, there's a pony man," said Dina.

They saw a pony trotting behind a man who held its reins in his hand.

"Mother, may we have a pony ride?" asked Vicky.

"All right, but remember to hold on tight to the reins," said Mother.

Dina called out to the pony man. He came at once, with the pony trotting behind him.

Dina stroked the pony's head and said, "He looks so smart."

"What is the pony's name?" asked Vicky.

"His name is Tim," said the pony man.

"He's so big. How shall we get up on him?" asked Vicky.

"Put your foot on this, my boy," the pony man said to Vicky. "I'll help you up."

Then Dina got up behind Vicky.

Mother told the pony man to take them carefully.

"Don't worry, Ma'am, they'll be all right. Tim is very good with children," he said. He held the reins as Tim began trotting.

They went for a long ride along the shore.

"Look at the lighthouse," said the pony man. "Do you know what a lighthouse is?"

"Yes, it's a tower with a strong light," said Vicky. "It guides ships to the shore."

"That's right. You're a smart boy!" said the pony man.

Soon they rode along a part of the beach which was full of rubbish. There were empty bottles, cartons and cans everywhere.

"Just look at all this rubbish," said Dina.

"Yes, people come to have fun at the beach and leave all this rubbish behind," said the pony man.

"Dina, we must not leave any rubbish behind when we go home," said Vicky.

Terry wagged his tail and ran behind the pony, barking happily. He picked up a carton and began playing with it. Then he dug a hole in the sand.

"He wants to hide the carton in the sand," laughed Vicky. "Silly dog!"

"Now it's time to go back," said the pony man.

"That was a lovely ride. Thank you," said Vicky, as they got down from the pony.

Mother paid the pony man and thanked him too.

"You must be hungry again. Come, let's eat now," she said.

They had biscuits, fries, fruit and sandwiches for lunch. Then all of them had some orange juice.

Terry had some sandwiches too. Then he began to dig a hole in the sand.

"Stop it, Terry!" said Mother. "You're throwing sand on us."

"He thinks it's a game," laughed Dina. "He wants to hide his sandwich in the sand."

The sun was going down now. "Time to leave, children," said Mother. "Get dressed and put all the rubbish in this bag. We must leave the beach clean. Then pack up all the things."

Vicky picked up the pail and spade. Dina packed the beach ball, Terry's rubber bone and the napkins. Mother packed the beach towel.

"Come along, Terry, it's time to leave," said Vicky.

Woof! Woof! barked Terry. He wagged his tail and ran around them.

They walked along the shore, picking up seashells on the way.

As they got into the car, Vicky said, "Thank you, Mother, we had a great time."

"Yes," said Dina. "What a lovely way to begin our holidays. We must come again, and bring Father too."

What did Vicky and Dina make with the sand?

Why was Terry pulling the towel?

What is a lighthouse?

# Let's Read

# Fun at the Fair

The sun was looking in from the window. Sara and her brother Dan woke up very excited.

"Yippee!" shouted Dan, as he jumped out of bed. "Today is a holiday!"

"Yes, and Mother promised us that Father would take us for a ride in our new car," said Sara.

"I wonder where Father will take us," said Vicky.

She woke up Polka, her dog. Dan woke up Toffee, his favourite toy dog.

Mother came and asked them to hurry up.

"I am packing your breakfast. You can eat it in the car on the way to the fair," she said.

So that was where they were going! The children were excited.

"Yippee!" said Sara. "We'll have such fun at the fair." She took a fresh towel, rushed into the bathroom and started getting ready.

"Mother, may I have another tube of toothpaste? This one is over," she called out.

"Yes, here's a new one. Dan, come to my room," said Mother. "I'll help you wash and dress."

They hurried down the stairs. Sara took Polka along and Dan took Toffee. Father was waiting for them.

Dan was so excited that he dropped Toffee while getting into the car.

"Here he is," said Father, as he dusted Toffee and gave him to Dan.

Mother locked up the house and they soon set off.

Polka barked softly. He knew the children were excited, so he was excited too.

Mother gave the children their favourite peanut butter and tomato sandwiches.

Polka also ate quietly. He liked eating from Sara's hand.

Dan munched on his sandwich and looked out of the window. Soon they had left the town behind.

"Children, you must be careful when you eat," said Father. "Please don't make a mess in our new car."

After they had finished eating, the children listened to their favourite songs on the radio.

Suddenly Dan shouted with glee.

"There it is! The giant wheel! I want to sit on it, please."

"Yes, dear, you will," said Mother.

There was a long line of people at the ticket counter.

Father and Mother stood in line while Dan and Sara looked at all the posters.

"Look Dan, they have elephant rides," said Sara. "Won't it be fun to ride on an elephant?"

"And there's a camel!" shouted Dan. "I want to ride on the camel too."

Polka was running up and down the line and barking in excitement. A little boy got frightened and began to cry.

"Polka, come back here!" said Dan.

"Don't be frightened," Sara said to the little boy. "He's only barking because he's excited."

Polka wagged his tail and stood quietly next to Sara.

When their turn came, Father bought tickets for everyone.

They went in and looked at the rows of stalls on both sides.

"Let us begin by looking at the stalls from this side," said Mother. "Then we won't miss out any stalls."

"Yes, that's a good idea," said Dan, when he saw that the first stall was selling pizzas.

"Father, may we have a pizza, please?" he asked.

"But you just had sandwiches in the car," said Mother, laughing.

"I am hungry again," said Dan.

Father bought a pizza for the children.

At the next stall, coupons were being sold for the rides. Mother bought some and gave them to the children.

"Listen to this!" said Father, looking at a poster. "There's a dog show in the afternoon. Sara, if you want Polka to take part, we have to give in his name at Stall 12."

"Oh yes, Father, please let's give in his name," said Sara.

Mother wanted to look at the things on sale at the next stall. So Father and Sara went to give in Polka's name at Stall 12.

Dan and Mother began looking at the things at the next stall.

"Let's buy this apron for Grandmother," Dan said. "It has two pockets. The last time we visited Grandmother, she baked brownies for us. I remember the pockets of her apron were coming off."

"That's a very good idea, Dan," said Mother.

Thinking of brownies made Dan hungry.

"Mother, please let's have some candy floss," he said.

He pulled Mother to the next stall that was selling candy floss. Mother bought candy floss for everyone. Just then, Father, Sara and Polka came back.

Polka was sniffing the candy floss, so Mother bought him some. As soon as Polka bit into it, it melted and got stuck on his nose.

Polka could not understand where the candy floss had gone. He barked and once again tried to eat it. The sticky candy was tickling his nose. The children had a good laugh.

It was beginning to get hot.

"I'm thirsty, Father," said Dan.

"There's a lemonade stall," Father said. "Let's go and have some lemonade."

Dan drank his lemonade and looked around him.

"Mother, let's go on the giant wheel next," he said. "Oh, but there's such a long line."

"I have an idea," Mother said. "I'll wait in line while you have a ride on the merry-go-round."

Dan and Sara went for a ride on the merry-go-round. When they got off, Father said, "Hurry up. Mother is calling us. I think your turn on the giant wheel has come."

Sara got on to the giant wheel with Mother.

Polka wanted to get on too. He barked and tried to get in with Sara and Mother.

The man at the counter said, "I'm sorry. Dogs cannot be taken into the giant wheel."

Father took Polka to one side and said, "Wait here quietly."

Polka barked softly, wagged his tail and waited quietly.

"Poor Polka," said Sara.

Father came back and got in with Dan. By the time the giant wheel filled up, they had reached the top. They could see everything that was happening at the fair.

"There's the camel, Dan," said Father. "Look, some children are getting up on it to have a ride."

"See, Mother, the stage is being set up for the dog show," said Sara.

"And there's the elephant," said Dan. "Father, may we go for an elephant ride?"

"We'll see, Dan," said Father, smiling. "Let's do one thing at a time."

"Yippee! We're off!" shouted Sara, as the giant wheel began to move.

Some children began squealing and screaming at once.

At first the giant wheel moved slowly. Then it went faster. Up and down and backward and forward it went. And every time they came down, they could see Polka jumping and wagging his tail in excitement.

"Ooh, my stomach feels so funny," squealed Sara.

Many other children were laughing and screaming. Then the giant wheel came to a stop and everyone got off.

"Can we have another ride, Mother?" asked Dan.

"No, Dan, if we don't hurry, we will be late for the dog show," Father said.

"Oh yes, Father, let's go to Stall 12," said Sara. "They've set up a stage for the dog show there."

They all hurried to the stage. A man hung a card with a number around Polka's neck.

"Please wait near the stage," he said to Sara. "When I call out your number, you may come to the stage with your dog."

Sara sat on a chair near the stage with Polka on the chair beside her. Father, Mother and Dan sat in the front row.

Many other people came and sat down to watch the dog show.

Soon the dog show began. The man called out the numbers. One by one, all the dogs came on to the stage and showed what tricks they could do.

When it was Polka's turn, Sara asked him to dance. Polka started jumping up and down and round and round, while Sara clapped her hands.

Suddenly Polka stopped and began barking loudly.

"What's the matter, Polka?" asked Sara.

Polka left the stage and ran towards a man who was trying to hurry away. He wore torn clothes. He put something into his pocket but it fell down as the pocket was torn. It was a bracelet. Polka picked it up quickly with his mouth and ran towards Sara.

Some men caught the thief who had stolen the bracelet.

"That's my bracelet," said a lady standing nearby. She took it from Sara, thanked her, patted Polka and went away.

"This dog is very clever, and brave too," said one man.

"Yes, he must get a special prize," said another man.

It was getting late and there was still so much to see. The children ran to a stall where there were many toys placed in rows.

"Come and buy a coupon," the man at the stall was saying. "You will get five hoops. You must try to throw a hoop around any of these toys. If you can throw a hoop around a toy, then that toy is your prize."

"Oh Father, please buy us a coupon," said Sara.

Both of them tried to throw their hoops around the toys.

It was Dan's lucky day. He threw the hoop around a teddy bear.

"This is Polka's prize for being so clever," said Dan.

Next they went for an elephant ride. The children squealed as the big elephant began moving. Everything looked so small from their seat high up on the elephant's back.

"We must set off for home now," Father said.

As they drove out of the car park, Polka saw a man selling ice cream. He began barking and wagging his tail.

"Mother, I think Polka wants some ice cream," Sara said.

"And so do I," said Dan.

"Well, Polka must get an ice cream for being such a brave and clever dog," said Mother.

She got out of the car and bought all of them some ice cream. Then they set off for home.

Sara held Polka's ice cream while he licked it quickly.

"Be careful," said Father. "Don't make a mess."

"Mmm, that was lovely," said Dan.

"Yes, we had a lot of fun at the fair," Sara said. "Polka had fun too. Mother and Father, thank you for a lovely day."

What did Mother buy for Grandmother?

What did Polka do at the dog show?

What did the children see from the
top of the giant wheel?

# Let's Read

# The Accident

It was getting late. Rob wanted to go home. But the twins Sheila and Steve wanted to go on playing.

"Mother has taken Grandma to the doctor. Then she has to go to the market," said Sheila.

"Yes," said Steve. "And Father will be home late. So we can play for some more time."

"All right," said Rob.

They went back to the park to play.

Rob kicked the ball high into the air. The twins ran to head it. Steve stepped on one of the bricks that someone had carelessly left there. He lost his balance and started falling. He tried to hold on to something.

Sheila was close by. When Steve held on to Sheila, she too lost her balance and fell face down. Both cried out in pain.

Rob heard them cry out and ran towards them. He saw that Steve had fallen on Sheila. Steve was slowly trying to sit up. He was not hurt badly.

After sitting up, Steve turned to help Sheila. She too was trying to sit up. Her head had struck against one of the bricks. She had a cut on her forehead. It was bleeding.

Sheila put her hand to her head. It felt sticky and wet. When she saw the blood on her hand, she got scared. She began crying loudly.

Seeing the blood, Rob and Steve also got scared. Rob folded his handkerchief and pressed it on the cut.

"Don't cry, Sheila," said Rob. "Try and get up so that we can go home."

When Sheila tried to get up, she fell back. Rob told Steve to hurry up and get some help.

Steve ran home to find Father waiting inside. He had come home early.

"What's the matter, Steve?" he asked. "Why are you in such a hurry?"

"Father, Sheila got hurt when we were playing football in the park. She has a cut on her forehead. Rob has placed a folded handkerchief on it to stop the bleeding. He told me to get help," said Steve.

"How did she cut herself?" asked Father.

"She fell on a brick and hurt her head," said Steve.

"Come along with me. Let's take the first-aid box and see what can be done. If the cut has stopped bleeding, it is fine. Otherwise we will have to take her to the hospital," said Father.

Father got the first-aid box from the kitchen. He opened it to check if it had everything he needed.

"Let me see ... cotton, scissors, bandage, antiseptic lotion and cream – yes, everything is here," he said.

"Hurry, Father," said Steve. "They are waiting for help."

"Yes, Steve, I'm ready. Just take a bottle of water along so that we can wash the cut," said Father.

Steve took a bottle of water and they hurried to the park. Rob was waiting for them. When Sheila saw her father, she started crying.

"No, no, my little doll, don't cry," said Father.

"You'll be fine soon. Let me see the cut ... we have to clean it first and then dress it."

"Dress it ... what does that mean, Father?" asked Steve.

"Well, it means that after cleaning the cut with an antiseptic lotion, we apply the cream and then bandage it," said Father.

Father carefully washed the cut and then cleaned it with a ball of cotton and antiseptic lotion. He put some antiseptic cream on it and tied a bandage around Sheila's forehead.

"There, that's done," said Father. "Your cut is cleaned and dressed."

"Father, my head hurts so badly," Sheila sobbed. "I feel dizzy too."

"That's because you have lost some blood. I'll carry you home," said Father. "Don't worry. When we reach home, you can have your favourite orange juice."

"Steve, please pack up the first-aid box and carry it," said Father.

Steve put the cotton, antiseptic lotion and cream back in the first-aid box. Father lifted Sheila in his arms and Rob took the ball. They set off for the house.

"Just a minute," said Father. "Rob, please pick up these bricks and put them behind those bushes. Someone else may get hurt while playing."

"Yes, leaving these bricks here was a very careless thing to do," said Rob, as he picked up the bricks and put them behind the bushes.

It was getting dark. They hurried out of the park and went home.

When they reached home, Father very gently put Sheila on an armchair.

"Rob, please get some cushions," said Father.

Rob got some cushions and placed them around Sheila to make her comfortable.

"Thank you," said Sheila.

"Boys, please get me some wet towels," said Father.

Rob and Steve got some towels and a bowl of water. Father then wiped Sheila's arms and legs and face with the wet towels. This made her feel much better, but she was still in pain.

"Father, my head still hurts," she said.

"Take this medicine and try to rest. The pain will be gone soon," said Father.

Father measured out some syrup in a cup.

"Does it taste nice?" asked Sheila.

"Well, I don't know," said Father as he gave it to her.

"Ugh! It tastes awful!" said Sheila.

Father laughed and kissed her.

"It may taste awful, but it will make the pain go away," he said.

Steve was feeling bad. He stood by the window and said to himself, 'It's all my fault. If I had listened to Rob and gone home when he told us to, I would not have fallen and hurt Sheila.'

Father saw Steve standing quietly by the window. He went over to him and asked, "What's the matter, Steve?"

Steve turned to Father and began to cry. Father understood what he was feeling.

He hugged him and whispered softly, "It was not your fault, Steve. It was just an accident. It happens sometimes. But remember to be careful next time."

"Would you like to see some cartoons?" Rob asked Sheila.

"Oh yes, my favourite show must have just started," said Sheila.

The three children began watching the cartoon show.

"Does anyone want popcorn?" Father asked.

"Oh yes!" all the three children said together.

Father went into the kitchen to make popcorn for everyone.

"I just love cartoons," said Sheila. "They're fun to watch, aren't they?"

All of them laughed as they watched the cartoon show.

Father came in with a large bowl of popcorn. He was glad to see that Sheila had forgotten her pain and was enjoying the cartoon show.

"Popcorn for everyone," he said, and placed the bowl on the table.

"Mmm, I just love fresh popcorn, don't you?" said Rob, as he took some popcorn from the bowl.

"Father, you promised me some of my favourite orange juice," said Sheila.

"Oh yes, dear, I forgot," said Father. "I'll go and get it right away."

Father went back into the kitchen to get orange juice for the children.

Just then the front door opened and Mother came in. She was carrying many bags.

"I'm home," she called. "Will someone help me with these bags, please?"

Rob got up at once and helped her put the bags on the table. Sheila got down from the sofa and went to her mother.

Mother saw Sheila with a bandage on her forehead and cried out, "Sheila! What happened? How did you get hurt?"

She hugged and kissed Sheila. Then she picked her up and carried her to the sofa.

Father came out of the kitchen and said, "Don't worry, Marie. Sheila is all right now."

"I had a little accident, Mother," said Sheila. "I fell in the park while playing football and cut my forehead on a brick. Someone had carelessly left it lying there. Don't worry, I'm much better now."

"Oh, I'm so glad you're not badly hurt," said Mother.

"But I'm thirsty after all the popcorn," said Sheila.

"I was just making some orange juice for the children," said Father.

"I'll get the juice," Mother said. Steve went to the kitchen with her.

"Do you want to tell me something, Steve?" asked Mother.

"It's all my fault, Mother," he said. "Rob told us we should go home as it was getting late. But we didn't listen to him."

"Don't feel so bad, Steve. It wasn't really your fault. It was an accident," said Mother. "Now you've learnt to be more careful, haven't you?"

"Yes," said Steve happily. "And I've also learnt how to dress up a cut!"

"Dress up a cut?" asked Mother, as she smiled at Steve.

Father walked in just then and started smiling too.

"You mean you've learnt how to dress a cut," he said. Mother and Father laughed as Steve ran out.

"I have a new story to tell at school tomorrow," said Sheila. "I shall tell my friends all about my accident."

How did Sheila get hurt?

What did Father do when he saw Sheila?

Why was Steve feeling bad?